THE GIRL WHO BECAME A TREE

A Story Told in Poems by
Joseph Coelho

Illustrations by **Kate Milner**

Otter-Barry BOOKS

You have one saved message...

A STORY OF A GIRL

A story of a girl
with a hurt she can't express.
A tale of a creature?
A tail of deepest red.

A journey in a library
where a forest lurks.
A message that is stolen.
A fable of growing hurt.

THE LiBRARY

Its original use
overgrown in history.

The grey block-work,
a barricade of teeth.
The building is round,
wooden shelves line its rotundity
like ribs inside a vast torso.

It is a library
but also
    it is alive,
    it breathes,
    it is a wood.
    It is a forest.

Its shelves have been wrestled
from every type of tree
to house these books:
black Ebony entombs
The Horror.
Bright Pine hugs
The Poems,
black-brown Cedar wraps
The Mysteries,
as broad Oak clasps
The Histories.

The tables were hacked from Burmese Teak
to withstand all scratching.

It is a library but also not.
A library of knots.
Its heart always a murmur.
The rustling of pages
could be mistaken for leaves.

Whenever Daphne enters after school,
she takes three deep breaths
of the library's woody scent.
Listens for its pulse.
Closes her eyes and sees the forest
that's just a page-turn away.

THE LIBRARIAN

I never **really** chat to him.
I never really chat to anyone any more.
Teacher says, "You **need** to speak up,"
says, "If you need to talk to **someone**, I'm here."
But I don't need **to** do anything,
I don't need to **talk to** anyone.
The librarian always tries to talk.

The librarian.
Sets aside horror books for me,
ghost stories by MR J**am**es,
twisted **being**s by HP Lovecraft,
hauntings by Shirley Jackson.
The librarian **noticed** what I read.
The librarian got me talking.

The librarian.
Hands me a book of Greek myths,
tells me if **I** like horror
"You'll love these."
It's a book I **don't** want.
Tales of **transform**ations and angry gods.
The same copy
I'd read with my dad years ago.
I flip to Apollo,
a **cant**ankerous god of change,
of art and **heal**ing, music and lightning.

I find our page,
still dog-eared, the tale of Daphne.
Dad loved it cos of the tree.
I want my ghosts.

The librarian.
Stares with black beady eyes,
gives me another opt**i**on,
a huge battering r**am** book
about **monster**s in movies.
Tentacled monsters, things from the deep,
ghosts and ghouls.

I have a Hallowe'en **memory**,
a **can**dle-wax drip memory,
me and Dad
dressed up as a huge **creep**y Cthulhu –
Lovecraft's tentacle god.
I was **up on** his shoulders,
he was covered in st**u**ffed stockings.
It's like the librarian reads my thoughts.

I throw him a tiny smile,
take the book
and head to my corner.

DAPHNE

This is **D**aphne
fourteen ye**A**rs old
buried in her **P**hone thoughts
a latc**H**key kid
a frie**N**dless reader
finding sh**E**lter in the library.

Defined by her name,
at one with the library shelves,
awaiting Mum's return.

THE ARCHAEOLOGY OF WORDS

The glass display case holds me.
Brimming with the library's archaeology,
children of its foundations –
bog-wood seeping dark
skulls: prehistoric, fanged, huge.

Wolf skulls and hippo teeth,
sloths the size of bears,
things that lived here
when trees dreamed of inked leaves.

Incredible how all those animals
and the enormity of trees,
the unfathomableness of years,
could be stuffed behind glass.

Agnes shuffles past me.
She's always here,
always chatting,
always smiling.
The case hasn't caught her yet.

"You being good Daphne?"

She asks – her face all silver birch.
And before I can answer she peels...

"It's hard ain't it, it's hard to be good."

I hand her a small smile and wonder
what part of this moment will survive?
Whether words and kind deeds
leave traces in the soil.

DAFT-KNEE

My father was a tree surgeon
"Loves trees more than people," *said Mum*
"Not true," *he'd say*
"I've never hacked a limb off a person."

"Daft-knee!"
was the name the kids teased me with at school
they never knew
I was named to crown emperors.

"Daphne was turned into a tree
in Greek mythology."
My father tells me this story
"Trees are blessed with longevity," *he says.*

"You wish I was a tree,"
I tease
"Then you could lop off my limbs
whenever I chat back."

He always laughed
like the sun
"You've got it all wrong,
I protect trees."

"With a chainsaw?" *I giggle*
(He was always sharpening that thing)
"That's just for those tricksy trees,
the trees that are dead, dying or dangerous."

He'd come home smelling
of the trees he had healed.
Fresh as pine, earthy as oak.
We'd eat dinner to the aroma of the woods.

DAPHNE AND HER FATHER PENEUS

"You are growing older,"
said Peneus to his daughter.
Soon you'll run your course without
the comfort of my waters.

"I'll always meander near,"
said Daphne to her father.
"I'll deluge the course you carve,
my cascade will never falter."

"Just as my current winds
from tiny trickle to the sea,
you too must flow my love,
run your course without me."

"I'll never grow O-daddio,
our course will never change.
Daughter runs with father forever,
mirrored waters must stay the same."

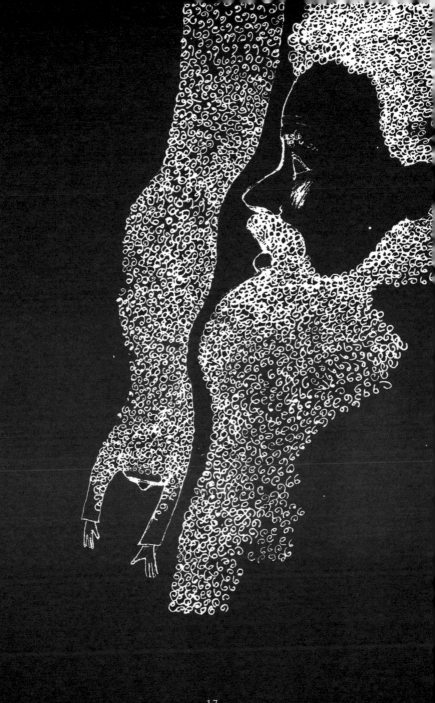

THiS LiBRARY IS
A FOREST

It's waiting in the tables
    wrestled from split ash trunks.
It's staring from the chairs
    carved from sanded beech branches.
It's listening in the pages
    teased from pulped birch bark.
It's sobbing in the pencil ends
    wept from rubber tree latex.
It's whispering from the ink
    bled from tumorous oak galls.

This library is a forest.
Rung in stories.

SHE COMES IN ALONE

Fingers
singly typing,
playing online.
Alone.

Before.
She'd cascade in here
with a swarm of friends,
crowding around the computers,
arguing over the boxsets,
discussing the latest series.

Now
she   sits
in   her   corner,
thinking,   reading   and   listening.

Alone.

On   her   phone.

Alone.

DELETED

Ping!
Ed
Daphne you ok?
Let's hang out!

-Deleted-

Ping!
Ted
Did you get Frawley's homework?
I don't get it... Please help :)

-Deleted-

Ping!
Dele
Hey Hun - You going to Dan's party?
Please say you can make it.
We've not hung out in forever.

-Deleted-

Ping!
Elle
Have I done something wrong?
Why aren't you picking up?

-Deleted-

PALM GAZER

I'm just staring
at my screen-palm.
A window on the world,
a finger-smudged cell within it.

Looks like I'm playing,
texting, messaging.
I'm just staring
at my screen-palm,
a window on the world,
a finger-smudged cell within it.

Scrolling the binge-videos.
The eye-rot.
I'm just staring
into my palm-screen,
a window on the world,
a finger-smudged cell within it.

Trying to peer out
at what lies ahead.

THE SECURITY
OF BOOKS

The offspring,
with lumberjack shoulders
and knots for eyes.
Dragged through a hedge
backwards.
Stand out like scarecrows in fields.

The offspring,
who need a break.
Who don't need to be told
"Sssshhhhhhh."

The offspring,
who are here because:
they have to be,
no one is home,
nowhere else is safe.

The offspring,
waiting for the flutter of a phone call
in the shade of a library.
The ones who depend
on the security of books.

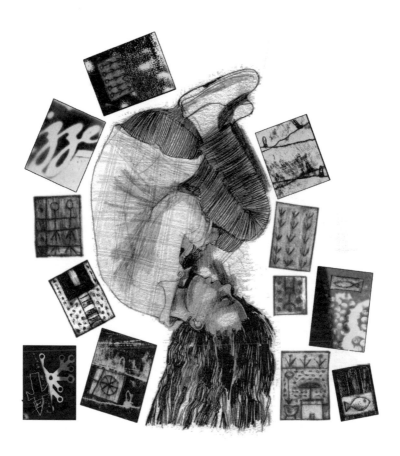

KEY

Yes of
course
I checked.
It wasn't
there...
No
because
you
used it
yesterday
because
you
forgot
yours
remember?
Yes you
did
Mum!
You
forgot
it again,
it's like

the fifth
time...
And on
Friday!
Yes you did!
You always do.
YES!
YOU DID!...
Dad wouldn't have forgotten...
Nothing!...
Fine...
Yeah.
The library don't shut till seven.
It's fine.
Yes...
I'm not hungry anyway...
Ok... Ok... OK...
Yeah I will...
YEAH I WILL!
YES
I SAID I WILL...
YESISAIDIWILLIGOD!
OK...OK.... OK....
BYE.

25

MUM

She comes home tired,
all eye-bags and blood-stains.
A slab of nothing
in the doorway,
bread won under each arm.

But I'm so angry
all the time
and she is all I have.
So I slip into fire.
Turn love into thistles.

EARBUDS IN

The sound of people eating,
their chomp chomping,
lip smacking,
tongue slurping,
makes me want to pack their teeth
with ocean foam,
with dried leaves
and bonfire.

People chatting
nonsense.
Loudly.
The aggravation
of only hearing one side of a conversation
makes me want to stuff their mouths
with their inflatable dartboard words.

Typing.
Tip tapping on a tiny keyboard,
a child-sized keyboard.
Plinky plonky typing
makes me want to fill their hands
with wet concrete.

So I stuff my ears
with earbuds,
cement them in
and let the sounds inflate
until I can't hear
their calls for me to remove them,
their hollow threats and empty teasing.
All silenced by sound.

THE LIBRARIAN'S TASK

So many books for you to borrow,
tales of woe and poems of sorrow,
words to make your heart churn.

I have one little question, a heavy task,
the fateful question that librarians must ask...
Do you have any books to return?

EARBUDS OUT

I wrap myself up in a song,
throw it over my head
and snuggle down into it.
Scrunch up my eyes
until nothing else exists,
just me and the song.

I'm floating in space,
tethered to a ship I can't reach,
tethered by a song.
I float,
breathing in the song,
floating in emptiness.

So when I'm asked
to listen,
to take out my earbuds,
(it sounds stupid)
but it's like asking me to
      Not Breathe!!!!
To cut off my lifeline,
whip back the covers
and see the creature.
To roll in the cold black,
to crash down to an exploding earth.

But you ask
(and I don't want to be rude).
So I take a deep breath of the song,
pump uncried tears into an inflated smile,
take my earbuds out.
And hunt in my bag for books.

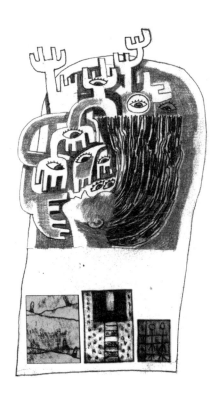

RETURNING

The world crashes in.
A tsunami of sounds
in this shush-filled space.

Nothing in my ears
to stopper the typhoon of thoughts.
I drip the books back.
The books that have soothed me...

"A Monster Calls"
"The Hidden Life Of TREES"
"Long Way Down"
"Will You Catch Me"

"Gossip From The Forest"
"Journey To The River Sea"
"The Song From Somewhere Else"
"Reality Is Not What It Seems"

MY CORNER

In the corner
between fantasy and fact,
skirting myth and magic.

There's a table,
different and distinct.
An old desk for writing and reading.

The librarian
reserves and reveres it
with a little and lonely sign.

"For quiet study
for quiet conceptions
for silent reading
for silent assumptions."

Room for one,
it has a sleek and sloped top
for jotting dreams and delusions.

The desk travels
in my cornered and cluttered mind.
Between fantasy and fact,
hemming myth and magic.

I find myself lingering there
more and more.
Scratching my dreams
into its undying and unifying surface.
Inking fantasy into fact,
shading magic with myth,
wanting things to thaw.

Wishing change could comfort,
knowing change only constricts.

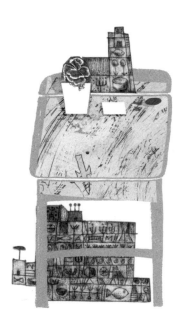

DESK

Who wrote on you?
All those years ago,
who studied your curves and spirals?

Who picked you out from the shop?
Who squealed with glee when you arrived?
Filled your ink-well
and wrote on you?

Who wrote on you?
Who scratched their marks
into your varnish?
I hate them for it.
Stupid tags,
names and hearts
and wounds.

I run my fingertips over your scabs,
wishing to heal them
(though I know that doesn't work).
Tracing your gouges.
It's like tracing your bark.
Closing my eyes
I see the full height of you,
your calligraphic branches
and lettered leaves,
your sap-ink.

Your treeness breathing
into my fingers and palms,
a forest of stories
contained in the grain of your history.

DAD'S SICKNESS

If I wore
my history on my skin.
You would read of sickness
spreading thin.

A sickly pale
a translucent skin
that my family are trapped within.

CUPID – DRAW BACK YOUR BOW

Eros would saunter,
bow clenched in loving hand,
arrows feathered in finest flock.

Tips dipped in:
golden heart-ache,
leaden desirelessness,
silver fancies
and bronze devotion.

He'd peacock around,
winking at the gods,
biting his lips
through dog whistles.
A cheeky smile
framing those lust-white teeth.

Apollo would thunder
as he watched:
lyre tuneless by his side,
trousers paint-splattered,
bow jostling with a stethoscope
around his neck.

The jealousy

zapped out of him,
faulting Eros' archery skill,
belabouring Eros' points,
Apollo's arrows all aquiver.

But Eros
is all about love – man,
he's laid-back – dude.
This volley of words
bounces off him.

Eros nocks,
          aims
          and shoots...
Apollo deep in his heart
with gold.

APOLLO

My father was a tree surgeon,
loved everything forest or wood.
Taught me how to carve my first flute,
made me memorise the names of trees
on the way to school.

"The trees with the club-shaped leaves
of brilliant green are lime,"

he'd say, pulling a bunch
and popping them into his mouth.
"They're edible."
He'd smile with the slime green showing
between his teeth,
chasing me until I screamed.

"Daphne was turned into a tree
in Greek mythology."

My father tells me this story.
Tells me how Apollo
chased her, hunted her,
was in love with her.

"There are many theories
but I think gods are symbols.
Apollo represents healing and the arts,
music and the hunt.
That god is all about life,
all about change,"

He says and I laugh.
Tell my father how I'd kick
Apollo in the nuts,
shoot him with his own arrows,
show him the meaning of thunder.

"That's my girl.
I wish some things didn't change
but all things do,"

says Dad.

"And change can hurt."

PHONE GONE

My bag is endless.
My pant pockets are pits.
My coat a Rubik's Cube of folds,
turning out tissues,
scrunched receipts,
a pencil sharpened down to the butt,
a leaking biro.
An acorn?
My old earbuds – the pink tangled ones,
chewing gum smudged in a silver wrapper,
a scrap of paper with Mr Smith's homework
written on it.
A flyer for a demonstration,
everything...
but my phone!
My rose-gold phone.

No phone!
No phone!
(Where is it?)
No Phone!
(My Photos)
No Phone!
(My Music)
No Phone!
(Mum's gonna kill me)

No Phone!
(My Messages)
My Phone!

Gone.

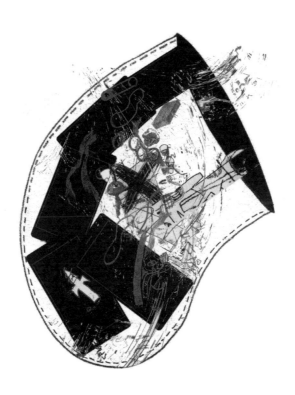

OUTCRY

W hy did I shout that?
H e turned red I swear!
E veryone turned around
R eading stopped!
E veryone glared.
S tupid to shout.

M um says, "Swearing is a filler for bad vocabulary."
"Y eah Mum – I'll remind you of that next time you stub
your toe."

* ear soaked me as soon as I said an
* xpletive. Understand! I don't normally swear.
* an't go anywhere else – Mum's not back till seven.
* ids have nowhere to go once it gets dark out.
I am just a kid... when it suits me.
N o way the librarian's gonna let me stay.
G earing up to chuck me out...

P robably calling the police.
H elp! Sweaty teen in Horror section.
O nly chance, act hurt, like I got cut, or fell.
N o one can blame me for swearing if I'm hurt.
E yes, please cry now, come on... the librarian is coming
over.

EVERYTHING OK?

He's got this evergreen smile
like a kid
trapped in the trunk of a man.

And it doesn't matter that I can't weep on cue
can't get the 'poor me' veneer into action
cos straight away
I know it doesn't matter,
I swear
he chuckles as he says...

"Everything OK?"

49

CREATURE

His smile fades,
I swear a breeze blows through the library.
That smell I always liked
gets stronger.
It's not booky,
it's earthy.

He looks at me serious.
The nectar gone from his eye.
I can't help but notice how hairy his ears are,
how small and black his eyes.

He gazes down at me,
dead serious
and says...

"A creature took your phone. Follow the nuts."

NUTS

He's flipped.
Gone crazy.
Wacko.
Off his rocker.

And I'm...

Not in the mood.
Haven't got the time.
This is no time for jokes.

I want my phone.

But there's something
about the way he is staring
and the chill in the room
and the fact that everyone else
seems to be moving slowly,
like slow-motion,
like for them – time has slowed.

And then I look down

    and
            see
                    a
                        trail
                            of
                                nuts.

FOLLOW THE YELLOW BRICK ROAD

They're laid out ahead of me
                A trail of nuts
                        ("Am I going nuts?")
                A maze of macadamias
        A path of pecans
A boulevard of brazils
            A walkway of walnuts
        ("I think I'm definitely going a bit nutty")
A cascade of cashews
    A haze of hazels
        ("What madness is this trail seeding?")
            Will this journey of crazy
                This impenetrable shell of mad
                    Open up the secret to what I have lost?

HAiRY

I have sat cross-legged
savouring sentences,
tasting novels,
scrumping the juiciest reads
in this library;
biting and discarding,
hungry for flavour.
A sweet introduction here,
a salivating description there,
a crisp cliffhanger,
even the odd spoilt ending.

I rocket along the trail
and start to feel light,
the light starts to dim.
The dimples of light
from the windows
above the belts of shelves
are starlight pinpricks.
I continue on
past... **The Astronomy Section.**

The carpet is thicker now,
each step sucking into the ground.
I track the trail,
the damp smell of earth and leaves
as I leave... **The Nature Section.**

The hairs on the back of my neck
are prickling.
Grave footsteps.
I'm sweating.
Fringe sweat glazed to my forehead,
arm hairs, minuscule soldiers – terrified.
Head down following,
past... **The Anatomy Section.**

I find a tuft of matted hair,
red-flecked,
coarse and stinking.
Where the books are leather-bound mummies.
The shelves are rougher, thicker and marked
with notches...

teeth marks!
right by... **The Horror Section.**

A pile of books
have fallen from their shelf.
Tossed from their shelf!
Revealing a hole in the wall,
a large ragged hole into blackness,
just large enough
for a curious girl to crouch,
in a section that is.... **Unmarked.**

LEAD iN THE HEART

Apollo plucks
the gold tip
from his heaving heart.
A red river runs rivulets
down his chest,
down each paint-smeared bullion leg,
tinkles onto the ground,
runs to the feet of a river girl.

This daughter of Peneus
is all swells and salt air
all sea-spray and white-water.

Their eyes meet.
Just as Eros prepares his arrow
with a smelter's grasp...
 nocks,
                    aims
                              and shoots
                                        a tip of lead

into the girl's crashing heart.

GRUB-LIKE

A worn hole lies in the middle
of the russet bookcase.
Worn smooth by what?
Scraping feet? Dragged bodies?

The worn hole leads to a tunnel,
through which Daphne squirms.
Grub-like.
Lit by a crisp illuminance,
a golden deliciousness that tempts.
In her core she knows something isn't right.

The floor is crunchy:
twigs, sticks, half-chewed nuts.
Various pippins.
The empty caps of acorns,
the spiky shells of horse chestnuts,
the dark brown skins of conkers,
the peeled petals of beech kernels.
All nibbled.

Nut shells crack
underneath Daphne's
old dirty white trainers
(Dad used to buy the trainers)
in a gala of bursts.
She inches her way
granny slow,
down the rotten tunnel.

Getting her shirt dirty.
A man's orange shirt,
far too big for her but she likes it,
likes how it smells.
Her mother
could never stop her wearing it,
could never stop her dirtying it.

"The apple doesn't fall far from the tree," she'd say.

A TRAIL OF MEMORIES

On she writhes
    through the tunnel.
        Leaving the library behind.

           A plastic games cartridge.
           (Button mashing with Dad)
           Pressed into the mud.

"This is ancient,"
Daphne thinks.

On she writhes
through the tunnel.
Leaving the library behind.

           Faded Instax photos.
           (Pulling silly faces with Dad)
           Litter the twigs.

           "I know these,"
           Daphne breathes.

On she writhes
through the tunnel.
Leaving the library behind.

A pair of size twelve work boots.
(Learning to dance on Dad's toes)
Scuffed at the tunnel's end.

"It can't be!"
exclaims Daphne.

Clutching the shoes to her chest
as if trying to place her heart
within them.

INTO THE WOODS

Trees
taller than the library,
taller than the Clock Tower in town,
taller than the Cathedral!
Taller than her eyes could take in.
Taller than her father.

So tall their tops grazed heaven.
Wider than the hug of her entire class,
so thick that roads could be cut through them.

A path wound through this towering forest,
A well-trod, well-dragged path.
A path where the grass daren't reach.
A path littered in mounds of stuff.
The columns of computer consoles.
spires of marbles, jelly-sweet monoliths,
wrapped chocolate bars forming steeples.
A temple of the outstretched arms of dolls.

A mess of hoodies (mostly red).
A spoil of golden balls.
And nuts, lots and lots
of half-gnawed nuts.
Making ridges and cliffs,
elevations and precipices.

Daphne follows the trail,
where flowers have no head to grow,
until she sees a sparkling, a shining.
A hut! Tiny.
Shimmering in the sickly forest light.

A forest of past memories
lies in wait for all of us.
A place where earth and dried seeds,
dead wood, teeth and fur conspire
to get us all lost.

IN A WOOD NEAR YOU...

Take a walk in any forest,
wood or copse
in 'the sticks'
or the edge of town.

Search long and deep enough,
let your feet guide you
and memory lose you.

You'll find a structure like this one,
the shadow in which
Daphne now stands.

A misshaped thing
fitting and out of place.
Wrong and absolutely right.
Remembered and never seen before.

For Daphne
it was barely bigger
than the curtain-defined space
of a hospital bed.
Built of gadgets.
Cables threaded its sides,
buried themselves
deep into the earth like drips.
Circuit boards and buttons,

keyboards and beeping screens
littered its surface.
Along with phones!

Mobile phones:
crumbling iPhones,
archaic Blackberries,
grizzled Nokias,
exhausted Motorolas,
petrified Kindles,
aged X-boxes,
fossilised Commodores.

As she kicked at the
buzzing beeping construction

she failed to hear
the paw steps approaching.

A TIP OF LEAD

A tip of lead
in the heart
spreads.

Pencils down the veins
weights the guts
with the fear of change.

Apollo ran at Daphne,
gold sparks in his eyes,
his paint-explosion trousers
a rainbow blur.

The lead in Daphne's eyes
wanted only grey.
She fled like prey.

Apollo sped towards Daphne.
Gold dripping from his mouth.
Lyre strumming in hand.
A stringed cacophony.

The lead in Daphne's ears
wanted a molten hush.
She pushed through her rush.

Apollo flung himself at Daphne,
gold sweat dripping.
His stethoscope threatening to diagnose.

The lead in Daphne's blood
wanted no healing.
She ran to her father-river appealing...

Take my sheen
from his eyes
turn my form into wood
I have no need for colour
for music or science
I want nothing of change
hear my defiance
I wish to be rooted
to be truncated, laureled and lopped
I wish never to grow
I want everything to stop
to stay
to always be the same
my father's river-daughter
forever stuck by his waters.

HOC THE GRIZZLED CREATURE

Hit by the smell:
damp dog,
rotting leaves.
Rotten.

Thumped by the sight:
soiled fur,
squashed and bloody.
Roadkill.

Nauseated by the face:
the suggestion of a man,
battered and gory.
Monstrous.

Head-pounded by the stance:
the slump of the shoulders,
Quasimodo and gorilla.
Stooped.

Dizzied by the realisation...
a man-like squirrel creature,
rough leather-dressed,
covered in the fur of unknown animals,
their dried flesh
still attached in ragged patches.
Pockets bulging,
in places oozing.

Dumbfounded by the eyes,
gold-flecked and hooked,
baited and watching.

REAL FEARS

There are times
when what should scare us,
should pop our lungs
and pierce our hearts,
has no power.

When the most monstrous
is no more than:
a passing gnat,
a shadow,
a stain.

When? When we know
what truly scares us:
the emptiness of loss,
the heartache of death,
the soul wrench of lost sunsets
and star-robbed nights.

Daphne looks at Hoc
with mild surprise,
lifts a hand to her nose...

"You stink!"

ALL THE THINGS
IN BOOKS

WHAT IS A GIRL DOING HERE?
WHAT IS A GIRL DOING HERE IN THIS FOREST?
WHAT IS A GIRL DOING HERE IN THIS DARK FOREST?
WHAT IS A GIRL DOING HERE IN THIS DARK FOREST
WHERE THERE ARE MONSTROUS THINGS?
ANCIENT THINGS.

WHAT IS A GIRL DOING HERE
IN THIS DARK FOREST
WHERE THERE ARE MONSTROUS
THINGS?
ANCIENT
                THINGS.
THAT WANT YOU.

WHAT IS A GIRL DOING HERE
IN THIS DARK FOREST
WHERE THERE ARE MONSTROUS
THINGS?
ANCIENT
                THINGS,
THAT WANT TO
KEEP YOU HERE.

"WHAT KINDS OF THINGS?"

ALL THE THINGS YOU HAVE READ OF IN BOOKS.

READING TOGETHER (REMEMBERING)

She always smelt of outside
as her skin warmed
from her work walk.
We wrapped words
in the darkness.
The monsters kept in the ward
behind curtain and punch-card.
She left them on the hanger,
washed them from her scrubs.

"Been looking forward to this all day,"
she'd say
as she pushed the day's patients
behind forgetting.

"Nothing too scary," she'd plead
as I picked a book from the shelf,
something familiar,
something to get lost in.
We'd wrap up on the sofa,
telly on, sound down.
Me snuggled in her limb embrace.
Her arms showering over me
to turn the pages.

'COME READ WITH ME,' (REMEMBERING)

She'd plead
but I was always
one moment away from the next level –
zombie hacking,
outlaw shooting,
mutant splattering.

She'd sometimes tease me
with repeat reads,
the good old reads
from our snuggle down
mother-daughter days of ages ago.

But I'd always get angry.
I needed my lights and sounds,
needed everything to be busy.
Couldn't hack her kindness
or her shooting concern.

I JUST WANT MY PHONE

I don't care
about monstrous things,
ancient things,
things that bite, scratch or growl.

I just want what's mine.

I don't care how dark the forest,
how tall and gnarled the trees.
No matter how cold,
I'm brave, I'm bold.

I just want what's mine.

I'm not put off by sharp teeth,
no matter how long or yellow.
No mean sharp claws
will keep me indoors.

I just want what's mine.

I'll follow night into the forests.
Chase the moon when it drowns in the sea.
I'll scale a mountain
all the while shouting...

I just want what's mine.

DAPHNE TRAPPED

"*Stay and play*," said Hoc the grizzled Creature,
smiling through his yellow teeth.
Then he parted a curtain of trailing cables,
revealed what was underneath.

A bean bag of mole fur,
some heads still attached,
a filling of dried acorns
perfectly moulded to Daphne's back.

Screens covered every wall,
games consoles beeped.
Every adventure she could ever imagine
lay waiting for her to complete.

There were controllers for PlayStations,
X-boxes and old Sega Systems.
Daphne was an avid player,
there was no point in resisting.

She sat upon the moleskin bag,
each little mole head gave out a sigh
and she could swear she saw fear glint
in each little mole head's eye.

She soon forgot about her mobile
and the precious things it contained
and as if on cue the forest deep
started to blow and rain.

Inside the hut was dry, all the screens flashing,
she pressed START on the controller.
The grizzled creature's smile
got bigger, wider, bolder!

"Stay and play," he chittered.
"There's no rush, no mother telling you to stop!
Play until your heart's content,
get your score to the very top."

Daphne wasn't listening,
she was deep into her game-playing session.
The world around her faded away,
the grizzled Creature had known her obsession...

had known the right buttons to press
to stop this girl thinking.
The hut closed tight around her,
its roots would soon be drinking.

Soon they'd be sipping on this girl
to change her into something new,
for this hut was a terrible trap.
There was nothing Daphne could do.

ONLINE

I play computer
with my dad
online.

We're apart
but we connect
online.

Mum would say,
"Just an hour."
But she daren't make me whine.

His gamer tag is Lion-Oh75
cos he was well old
like one hundred and nine!

Mine is Unicornsparkles
cos I chose it when I was well young.
About eight or nine.

We built
memories together
online.

He lets me have the resources I need,
power packs and health –
all mine.

He would always say,
"What's mine is yours." And I'd reply,
"What's yours is mine."

It's not as good
as before, snug on the sofa,
vine and twine.

Better than nothing.
Not perfect,
far from divine.

A shadow of our life,
a game played with my father
online.

SCRAPE AT HEAVEN

My dad's Avatar
plain as day
materialising on the screen.

Beyond Belief!
Defying Possibility!
A Mesmerising Revelation!

The grizzled Creature, Hoc,
has a smoke-and-mirrors smile.

"Who knows what's possible
in a forest
where the trees
scrape at heaven."

GAME OVER

Hours a blur
Buttons beeping
Colours flashing
Defeated baddies
Puzzles solved
Hours pass
Saved lives

He helps me
I help him

He gives me health packs
I cover him
As he takes all the fire

And as I play
I forget everything:
The blur of appointments,
The beep of machines,
The dancing colours behind my eyes,
My defeated family,
The unsolved tests,
The never-ending hours,
The unsaved life.

HEARING HE WAS ILL

Hearing he was ill
felt fictional
my evergreen father
could never rot.

Dad and I filled our ears
with sap
sprinkled pollen onto our eyes.
We'd laugh it off
joke it through
our words all splinters.
Mum's words all pulp.
Her tears like woodworm.

*"If you believe it
you'll make it real."*

I thought
but my belief in miraculous cures
never set seed.

When bark is peeled
a tree swamps the wound
in sap
heals over thicker and scarred.

My sap was used up
in those monsoon months.
I healed over thick and harsh.

Mum left the wounds open.
Her sap always sparse.
She felt each cut to the core.

MOMENTS OF DISTRACTION

If I could replant those moments
of distraction
I'd lose myself
in a thicket of them.

If those moments could be grasped
I'd learn the knots of Giant Sequoia climbers
to tie those moments tight.

If moments of distraction
could be distilled and concentrated
I'd tap them.
Mist the air ahead of me with their oils.
Fold the scent in wax
and burn the candles to stumps.

Moments of distraction
are temporary
cut down before their prime.

The memory of you
always comes bulldozing in.

THE LAST BOOK

A book slams
into my lap.
Do the living have ghosts?
Startles me out
of my playing
like a shout in a library.
Pages flipped
to that watercolour picture...
The witch with the weeping mouth
and hungry eyes in her crumbed house.
The last book Mum and I
read together.

REMEMBER

Hunger burned first in her stomach
her lips felt leather-cracked
her mouth parched.

How long have I sat here playing?

Like waking from deep sleep
she started to remember
her mother
the library
the trail
the hole in the bookshelves
the creature.
Her father.
Her phone.

How long have I sat here playing?

Her eyes were strained
the screen was not the game
she thought, she dreamt, she imagined she was playing
it was all static fuzz.

How long have I sat here playing?

She tried to stand.
Vines and roots ripped from her legs.

How long have I sat here playing?

YOU CANNOT GO

You cannot go.

Said the Creature
as I arose from his strange nest to leave.

There are things that lurk in this forest
that'll make you weak to your knees.

His eyes glinted gold with their secrets
his maw drooled with his lies.

If you venture alone in this forest
you'll meet a deadly surprise.

The forest looked dark and foreboding
its leaves like talons and claws.

> *I must brave this dark forest*
> *for the phone I lost before.*

His laughless eyes pondered
a brand-new way to betray.

I'll search this forest for you
if you'll only sit and stay.

I knew it wasn't right
I knew that something was wrong
but I agreed to this trick of a devil
I swayed to the tune of his song.

Stay and listen by this hut,
make my nest your home.
Hear the melody of an old song,
and I'll return with your phone.

CHORUS

Familiarity haunts this place.
A hypnotism of reflections.
An enthralment of my own feelings.
The Creature leaves me with a song
more familiar than my own skin.

I'd laugh at Dad booming out
his tuneless rendition,
crooning louder as we approached school
to both embarrass and delight me.
We'd sing together,
I only knew the chorus.

I only knew the chorus.
Dad knew the whole thing.

The lichen-mapped stereo the Creature left
plays the chorus
on repeat
        over
            and over
                and over.

HOC'S SPELL

FOREST HEAR MY SPELL NOW.
TURN THiS GiRL WHiLST SHE WAiTS NOW.
DRAiN FROM HER ALL DREAMS NOW.
SiNK HER DEEP iN THE EARTH NOW.
HEAR OLD HOC'S SONG NOW.
GiVE HiM WHAT HE NEEDS NOW.
SO MY KiNG WiLL SEE NOW
HOW GOOD A SLAVE I CAN BE NOW.
THOUGH DREAMS BE BUT CRUMBS NOW
OF A SOUL'S FULL FEAST NOW.
THESE DREAMS WiLL BE ENOUGH NOW
FOR MY CRY TO BECOME A GROWL NOW.

WAITING

I'm told to wait and wait I will.
I'm pacing this old forest waiting for spring.
This tree-slow patience takes deathly skill.

I'm a bramble of fidgets, a girl-shaped anthill,
my hopes tied with matted-fur string.
I'm told to wait and wait I will.

My eyes search the canopy, taking their fill
of dreams, my expectations ring.
This tree-slow patience takes deathly skill.

I want to act, shout and scream, I want to over-spill
to show the twisting vines I am action's offspring.
But I'm told to wait and wait I will.

I'm feeding hours into time's sawmill,
doubt unfurls, distrust becomes a sapling.
This tree-slow patience takes deathly skill.

My fidgets are blooming, I won't sit still,
I must choose my own song to sing.
For now, I'm told to wait and wait I will.
Tree-slow patience takes deathly skill.

THE DEVIL FINDS WORK FOR IDLE HANDS

My father would warn me
"The Devil Finds Work For Idle Hands.
So Make Friends With Curiosity."
My father always warned me.

So whenever a problem finds me
and I'm lost in strange lands
I remember that my father warned me
"The Devil Finds Work For Idle Hands.
So Make Friends With Curiosity."

A CURIOUS CLIMB

The tree's bark was smooth
skin smooth
its branches elbowed low
so Daphne climbed high
curious to get a view
over this odd forest world
where creatures
have weird nest-huts
guts filled
with the latest
computer games and consoles
where she is consoled
by a father who
couldn't possibly be playing.
A father lost to her
who stirred
in this strange tree place.
She climbed until face to face
with a gnarl in the bark
a mass of worm-wood and knots
her stomach knotted
as the bark
arced, turned and twisted
arrested her gaze
and opened!

Two black ebony eyes
spied in the face of the tree!
It couldn't be!
She screamed and yelled
as she fell
into her hut
in a shower of nuts.

TREE MONSTER

Tree monster big
with its tree monster claws
tree monster mumbles
tree monster roars.

Tree monster twigs
on his tree monster head
tree monster shocking
tree monster dread!

Tree monster arms
twisted vines
tree monster trunk
a bark-skinned shrine.

Tree monster eyes
two ebony spheres
tree monster breath
an unholy frontier.

Tree monster sees me
in his tree monster sight
tree monster screams
will tree monster bite?

MONSTERS ON FILM

The monsters on film
don't come close
to real monsters.

The way your stomach
lurches to sickness.
The way your heart
stalks every beat.
The way your breath creeps,
the way your eyes
suck all the horror up.

Real monsters
become a part of you.

The monsters on film
have nothing
on real monsters.

FAINT

It's as if
sight
has a volume knob
which is turned down,
real quick.
And with it
colour and sound
and thought
and memory
and who you are
are all turned
down
to
    no
        thing
            ness.

HOW TO TURN A GiRL iNTO A TREE

TAKE ONE GiRL
OF 19 YEARS,
STEEPED iN MiSSiNG AND MOURNiNG.

TAKE FROM HER
WHAT SHE HOLDS DEAR –
A MEMORY OF A FATHER CALLiNG.

TEMPT HER FROM
THE WORLD OF BOOKS
THROUGH A TUNNEL OF FALSE PROMiSE AND DREAM.

KEEP HER HERE
WiTH LiGHTS AND SOUNDS,
DiSTRACT HER FROM THE EViL UNSEEN.

LET HER DESiRE
TO HOLD TiGHT THE PAST,
REACH DOWN iNTO THE GROUND.

LET HER REGRET ROOT,
LET HER SADNESS ENSNARE,
TO HER ANGER LET HER BE BOUND.

LET THE FOREST
DO iTS WORK
OF CHANGiNG THOSE TRAPPED iNTO WOOD.

LET THESE TREE-CHiLDREN FEED ME,
THEiR BiTTER FRUiT TASTES iNCREDiBLY GOOD.

I SHOT UP

I dream I ate the bread
and shot up.
Mum out of reach
by my feet,
so easy to ignore
with my head crowned in storm clouds,
my ears budded with hail.

I AM A TREE

When I was just a seedling kid
my dad would say, "Your head is hard —
like all hard heads that came before,"
and tap my head mock-hard.

My head now feels as hard as oak,
I try to free my eyes.
I swear I hear them creak and crack,
I'm tough but now I cry.

I try to rub my sappy tears,
my hands feel light and green,
they brush, whoosh and tickle my face.
Laughter replaced with screams.

I'm canopy, up in the sky,
crowns surround my branched head.
I cannot see my feet below,
my heartwood fills with dread.

My legs have gone! From two, to one.
One leg, one trunk, is me!
I cannot move, I'm rooted in.
I panic to get free.

I try to bend, to break, to stump.
I try to twist and turn
but all I do is shake and whoosh.
This wood I want to burn.

My hair a mass of mistletoe,
my skin is peeling bark.
I creak my eyes against their grain
as this forest turns to dark.

Dad always said, "Just count to ten
whenever shadows bloom."
I count my twigs and poll my sticks
but still I'm thorned by doom.

I am a tree, all trunk and branch,
my arms embrace the sky.
I am a wooden, sappy thing.
Who knew that trees could cry?

WHEN DAPHNE BECAME A TREE

Was Dad's favourite bit,
her changing,
her rooting in.

I hated it.
I wanted her to crash and storm,
hated the way she sank.

Asking her river father to be buried,
too scared of a mobile life,
a fighting life.

She should have raged
at Apollo.
And why does Eros get away?
He started it!

She should have shot him,
Apollonian-like,
with a splinter
of unrequited love.
She should have shot them both
before she ever dreamt of being planted.

Her father
should have wanted more
from her.

Should have expected more
from her.
God of raging white-waters,
god of tumultuous falls.
He should have expected deluges
from his daughter,
instead of running tears.

Seeing her turn
was my father's favourite bit.

I hated it.

DAPHNE

I shift and grow to stay still
my feet first root in shooting pain
fear of change takes deadly skill.

My skin thickens to my father's will
my mind has always followed the grain
I shift and grow to stay still.

I thought this pollarding would be a thrill
bones of agony is all I've gained
fear of change takes deadly skill.

Each unfurling leaf a fresh kill
every crack in bark a new way to maim.
I shift and grow to stay still.

Apollo tries to instil
a new love for stick, branch and cane
fear of change takes deadly skill.

This wood a prison, my scream shrill
locked into wood I'll stay insane
I sit and bow to stay still
fear of change takes deadly skill.

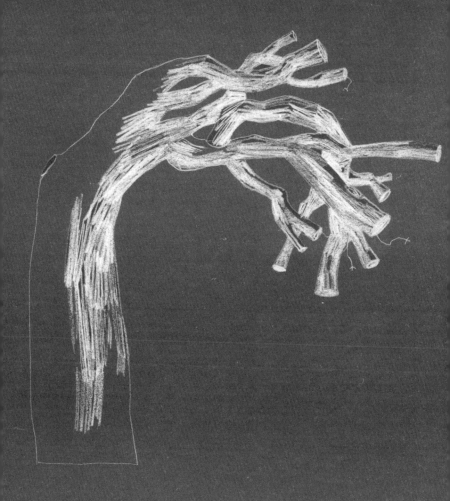

A FRiEND iN A MONSTER

I never would have guessed
that splinters could be kind,
that a tripping root can impress,
a rotten branch entwine.

Splinters can be kind
and a friend be found in a knot.
A rotten branch can entwine,
not all foes are enemies in a plot.

A friend was found in a knot,
a boy entombed in wood.
Not all foes are enemies in a plot,
though he scared me where he stood.

A boy entombed in wood,
a victim of believing,
he scared me where he stood,
his pining cry got me screaming.

A victim of believing –
tripped on a tale told to impress.
His pining got me screaming.
I never would have guessed.

LiViNG WOOD

This evergreen boy
is kinda cute
we make music in our branches
when we laugh together.

His name is/was
Euan.

He tells me things
about the Creature
(I speak tree now)
rustles to me
how the Creature
lures us with stuff –
a mulch to stake us in.

Thickens our blood to sap
cracks our skin
rings our bones
tree turns us.

"The young grow the brightest dreams –
when we are trees
our dreams are fruits
that the Creature gnaws."

BEHIND THE STUFF

The stuff by
his trunk is old:
mud-grimed cartridge consoles,
stone-smashed Gameboys,
rain-drenched PCs,
claw-scratched CDs,
bird-nested videos,
ant-infested Walkmans.
Ancient!

The stuff by
my trunk is new:
crisp PSPs ,
fresh Playstations,
unseasoned Xboxes,
untrodden ipads,
smartphones with every app.
Their screens not yet smashed to webs.

The old muddy tears
stormed at Mum
for refusing me the latest iphone.
Chills.

Euan's roots are threaded
through a forgotten VHS,
into the smashed screen
of a blank monitor.
A pair of abandoned red trainers
are half absorbed into his bark.

The thistled jealousy
I felt when some classmates
got ipads.
Rumbles a laugh
from deep within.

How stupid the stuff.
Collections of our sorrows.
Soulless detritus of our past.

The question behind
the stuff
falls out of me...

"How long have you been here?"

I STAYED AND PLAYED AND FORGOT

At the Creature's bidding
I stayed and played and forgot
everything and everyone at home.
I stayed and played and forgot.

The things they said,
strayed.
All the bad stuff
played away.

I stayed and played and forgot.
All was rot,
I was left all trunk and stick.

Sleep took me quick.
Roots hooked me thick
as I began to change outside and within.

I planted in,
tap-rooted in,
became a perch for birdsong.

The nails of my toes grew long,
dug into the ground strong,
my blood with sap transfused.

Then my legs fused,
bones and muscles diffused,
knees melding their caps.

Bark webbed my lap
and in my back
my spine grew beastly...

Into the branches above me.
Now no one can love me.
I am a tree-child.

A thing grown and wild.
A thing monstrously styled
by a creature of fear.

I've stood here
watered in tears
as he feasted on my dreams.

WORRY AND FEAR

I used to worry
that the things
that worry me.
always would.

That if I worried about
those worrisome things
weekday to weekend
they would always
worry me.

But I forgot them,
they slipped far afield
quietly.
Replaced by birdsong
and the drip of rain on leaves.

Now I fear
the things
I've forgotten –
my mother's fierce smile.
the fire of her cooked fare.
Did she ever say 'I love you'?

All have slipped
far afield
faintly.

Replaced by the knocking
of wood beetles and the hum
of moss on bark.

WORRY, AN AXE

Worry, an axe
over me, promising never to leave.
Revolving its claws, I feared its
rage, fearing I'd never forget, would always
yield.

Worry, an axe
over me, promising never to leave.
Revolving its claws, I feared its
rage but one day it
yielded.

Worry, an axe
over me, promising never to leave.
Revolving its claws, I feared its
rage. But one day it stopped.

Worry, an axe
over me, promising never to leave until I
realised its claws could retract.

Worry, an axe
over me, until I started to forget.

Worry, an axe
Worry – axed.
W.

FRIENDSHIP GROWS

We were blown together
windfalls of destiny
our friendship was all thundertooth
and back-slap
the playtime banter
of our autumn made twins of us.

We grew in the dirt
understood the mould on our soles
connected and fed,
never made crucifixes of our branches
we grew together
found ways to entwine
to protect and support
to rustle laughter
out of storms.

The tinkle of shared tears
watered at the root.

Turned us orchard
made us forest
kept the lumberjack at bay
in this way
we grew together.

A MOTHER'S LOVE

Trees breathe
with their whole bulk
from root-tip to crown
I take a breath
in a billion tiny gasps
and each stoma smiles.

Trees think
with every cell in their being
from bud-tip to anther
I stop thinking a billion tiny thoughts
and my sap rises.

And in the amber of my thoughtlessness
I see Mum,
Mum and me
clawed in silence
together grieving alone.
I see us stuck
her mouth honey-filled
mine stung shut.

I wish I'd read with her
when she asked
wish I smiled when she tried
wish I could have stopped
to breathe,
to see
the Amazon of her love.

A PHONE RINGS DEEP IN THE FOREST

From the depths
of the darkness,
carrying over the
buttons of moss
and the aerials of twigs.
A sound shocks.

It fizzes in the air,
vibrates through the trees,
causes gasps to mist
from their flaking jaws.

Birds radiate from the branches:
crows and ravens
with 'out of battery' eyes,
jays flashing
their wallpaper of blue.

A noise at once
terrifying and known.
The unmistakable trill
of a mobile phone.

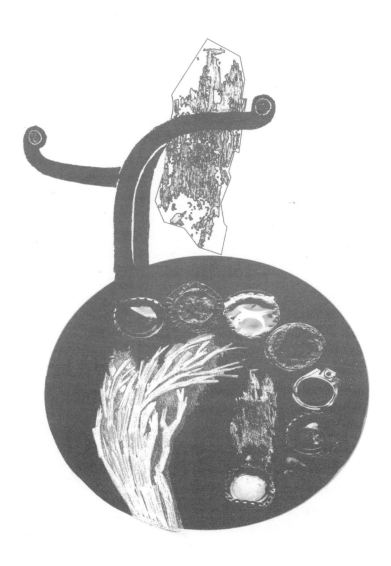

TREE MONSTER 2

How long have I stood here?
Rooted here?
Inactive.
Content with growing,
content scrolling.
Has it been moments or months?

Time creeps differently
when sadness
hardens your heart.

A creature
lured me here,
took my phone!
Said he'd get it back
(lied)
turned me into a tree
(idiot),
to eat my fruiting dreams
(sicko).

Euan says there's no escape,
he's been here for years.
Says we're trees now,
says life as a tree is peaceful.
Says there's nothing we can do.

I'm not a tree!
That matted, rotten creature
made a mistake with me,
he didn't turn me into a tree,
he turned me
into a tree-monstrosity.

DAPHNE IS MONSTROUS

All my leaves fall in a shower of weepings,
abandoning the raw nerve of branches.

Limbs become the angular click-dance of witch fingers.
Pawing the night of the wood and glow of the moon.

The anger that rises is thick and sweet,
sucking a river of force out of the loam.

Summoning something deep and dark right up
    from my trunk.
Letting it capillary through me, letting it be me.

And as my bark falls in Plane London sheets, leaving me
    raw in places,
a grin finds my crack of a mouth as the pain creaks to my
    core.

But still I'm still, coffin wood, timber entombed.
I'll never doubt that trees silently scream. But that sap is
    hot

and living wood is malleable, a branch twists and
    a stick turns,
suppleness rubbers through, makes Manchineel and
    Bunya of me.

Turns my limbs tentacle, makes the sawdust of my
     breath ooze,
from which woodworm fall. Each twig a claw, every
     splinter a tooth.

And I'm outside howling leaving Mum alone within.
I'm night-time stalking refusing the daylight glare of
     hospital corridors.

Am I a monster of a girl? A beast of a daughter?
I plunder my feet from the compost deep, split my trunk
     in two

and let my dark sap run, climb out of my hole with
     monstrosity on my mind
and go walking, walking through the forest deep.

No longer girl, if ever I was? I have grown into myself,
matured into my prime, realised the poison of my fruit.

WHAT ABOUT ME?

I've been alone
for time
that refused to tick.

Trees can live
without their cores
it's their thick skin
that keeps them going.

I learnt loneliness
in the abscission
of family and friends.

Found peace
in the company of one.
Made the stars
my companions:
they twinkled at every joke.
I whispered secrets
to the scents
of honey blossom and lavender
that they could never
let slip.

I found comfort
in the wind:
she would listen
with breezes
and empathise
with storms.

But...
the stars held
elevated conversations
that I couldn't join.
Aromas wafted where
I was unable to follow.
The wind's banter would often dictate.

Then you arrived
with your laughter and smiles
and anger and fury
and bad habits and beauty.

And the world grew.
My centre
started to fill.

And now you're
leaving.

Monstrous

The words tentacled out of me
"I'm not like you."
Frothing too quick to grab back
"You're sad and pathetic."
I swarmed unable to stop
"I don't want to be weak like you."
Each insult more grotesque than the last
"It's your fault you're alone."
A woodpile of put-downs as I stormed off to leave.
"You don't want a monster like me around."

My words had become fanged
I couldn't stop biting...
Throwing my fear,
             my anger,
             my sadness
at a friend – who didn't deserve it
without the means to flee.

Monstrous.

FOLLOW THE RINGING

I am rage,
stone-cracker,
soil-despoiler,
copse-corpse maker.

So why is my stomach
frozen leaf mulch?

I am frenzy,
field-bomber,
hill-raker,
mountain-puncher.

So why are my eyes
winter mist?

I follow the ringing
in my head.
A sound too familiar.
Dial my regret
into my fury,
drop-call my sadness
into my temper.
Cold-call my guilt
and let it ring
as I pursue the ringing.

WHERE'S MY PHONE?

Daphne crashed
through the darkness.

WHERE'S MY PHONE???

Her split tree trunk legs
pounded through the mud.
Her branched hands
tossed boulders
sent birds into flight
made bears scamper.
Her terrible monstrosity
sent a shadow
of terror before her.

WHERE'S MY PHONE???

The ring of her phone
was getting louder
she was closing in
uprooting dead trees
like forgotten skeletons
combing through thorned bushes
kicking through fields
of fairy circle mushrooms
forcing rivers to change course.

WHERE'S MY PHONE???

Up ahead was a hill
crowned by a circle
of dead trees
their branches
pleading to the sky
begging for help.

WHERE'S MY PHONE???

Her voice echoed
through the cathedral
of dead trees.
Mixing with the taunting
of her phone.

Shocked – into silence.

The trees
were not just trees.

A SURPRISE IN THE CANOPY

Cathedral of white wood,
tombs of trees,
their trunks familiar,
vaguely human shaped,
some trunks cracked,
the wooden faces frozen.
Their mouths quiet slits.

Some in the circle had fallen,
become crumbled towers
for fungi to rent.

Not a cathedral:
a graveyard,
a spoil pile,
a cleared plate.

Each tree
grew from a pile:
one of carved wooden toys,
another of tin playthings,
one of musical instruments,
another of china dolls,
their faces cracked,
their eyes wild and open
or set in a lop-sided following stare.

One of the trees
was huge.
Its trunk broader than a building.
Daphne peered up its huge height.

Amongst the dead branches
sat a throne.

THRONE OF NUTS

Throne of nut shells
mud and sticks.
Arms of spiky horse chestnut
cases brown with age,
seat of hazelnuts
and the insides
of beech kernels.
A back of
acorn galls –
blooming like tumours.
The ringing
of the phone
was coming from the throne
and sitting in the throne
was Hoc.

DEAL WITH A DEVIL

GiRL, WHY HAVE YOU TORN
YOUR ROOTS FROM THE GROUND?

> You tricked me with dreams,
> had me fantasy bound.
> Creature, who were these faces
> now dead in the trees?

THE FiRST LOST I FOUND, GiRL.
THE FiRST TO FEED ME.
PLANT YOURSELF HERE, GiRL,
RiGHT NEXT TO MY THRONE.

> You have nothing I need,
> Creature, I want to go home.

WHAT ABOUT THE GAMES, GiRL,
THE GAMES YOU PLAYED WiTH YOUR DAD?

> That wasn't real, Creature!
> You're making me mad.

WHO KNOWS WHAT'S REAL, GiRL?
WHERE TREES SCRAPE AT HEAVEN'S GATE.
TELL ME YOUR SECRETS, GiRL,
THE THiNG FOR WHiCH YOU CAN'T WAiT.

I'LL MAKE iT REAL, GiRL,
WHiLST YOUR FLESH HARDENS TO WOOD
YOU'LL HAVE YOUR HEART'S DESiRE, GiRL,
THiS DEAL iS GOOD.

> But you'll feed on my dreams,
> Creature, leave me hollow inside.

THiS iS TRUE, MY DEAR GiRL.
DEAR HOC NEVER LiES.
BUT WHAT NEED YOU OF DREAMS
AFTER WHAT YOU HAVE DONE!
BESiDES, THERE ARE THiNGS YOU'D MUCH RATHER.
DEAR OLD HOC...
CAN BRiNG BACK YOUR FATHER.

A VOICE COMES THROUGH

The woods become
a loudspeaker.
Static rings
through every tree,
assaults the air,
hums through the mud.

Daphne crouches over,
her huge tree-body
knotted in terror and pain.
Her great leafy limbs
struggling to block
the whorls of her ears.

A voice is riding
the sound-storm.
A crackling,
familiar voice.

A voice of birthday surprise
and homework help,
of stupid jokes
and scraped knee bandaging.

The voice of a father.

THE VOICE OF A FATHER

Speaks to you
with a look.

Steel-bands
through your nonsense.

The voice of a Father

Underplays the bass
of authority
with the strings
of naughtiness.

Crescendos too loud
and knows nothing
of diminuendo.

The voice of a Father

Can static hum
in annoyance
and soothe
with baritone gravitas.

The voice of a Father

Echoes through your life,
sits conscious-like
on your shoulder
and whispers
wisdom.

Whether you heed it
or not.

You Have One Saved Message...

Hey Love, it's Dad.

Missed you again today.
Mum caught me up.
I understand. Must be hard.
I understand.

I didn't want
to see your grandmother in the
end, she was a cloud-buster woman
but in those ultimate days, so thin.

You'll see me
when you're ready,
your mum tells me you're ok.
And that's enough.

Anyway.
Mum says you're watering the tree,
every day, thanks for that love
they are tender at the start
got to get those roots established.

Hopefully we'll get apples next year.
Make your delicious crumbles,
I love your crumbles.
Even when you mixed the sugar with the
salt.

I thought it was nice.
Think you were onto something there.

Oh love....
My unique marvellous daughter.

Life is all right.
Don't let this change that for you.
Live it, really live it. It is
unexpected and magical.
Special.
And you are going
to have an amazing life
you're going to bring such beauty
into the world.
You're going to
fill it with blossoms.
How could you not.

Love you Sapling.

TIRED

Tired of being angry
tired of being sad
tired of the guilt
tired of searching
   for your remnants
   in stored photos
   archived emails
   in replies and likes
   buried in clouds
   and rammed into bits.

Tired of the corruption
of memory.

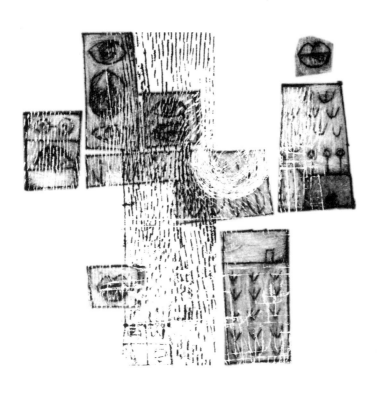

147

HEARTWOOD

The benefits of being a tree...

Heartwood at the core.
Stronger, richer, more potent.

My heart has widened and lengthened,
filled me from root-tip to crown.

Despite my claws and tentacles,
splinters and rage,
I feel different.

I am tree.
Heart running
through every part of me.

Despite the roar
that creaks through me.
I'm starting to feel free.

Heart-shell cracked,
something true spilling out.

Despite the ooze
I gurgle and drool
I feel soft and in control.
Hearing his message properly for the first time.

Despite the millions of replays,
despite listening in every class,
despite falling asleep to it at night.

I've only really just heard it.
Heard the love in it,
found the strength
to drop anger's veneer,
to leaf-drop guilt.
Heard the love
that rings through my family.

FATHER TREE

My father was a tree
whose full height
I could never climb.

Never far from his canopy.
I'm now deadwood surrounded.

Hunt me back his
evening promises,
his morning concern.

Dig me up his hug
on a frost-breath night.

Forage his jokes.
Nest build his laugh.
His faux shock and teasing.

I'm all peeled bark,
wept sap all over.
I'm all green shoots
and frost damage
and weeping willow.

The stuff
left behind
will never be enough.

Seed to his autumn,
sapling of his drop.
I hear his laugh in my core,
remember our moments
in the rustling of my crown.

The memory of his love
is enough.

SPECIAL OFFER

Hoc scuttles down
from his nutty throne
his head jerking
left and right
his black eyes
never leaving Daphne.
His bulging fur and oozing pockets
spilling crab apples
and walnuts, figs and medlars.

He approaches Daphne
slowly – all twitches.
She towers above him.

In one clawed grubby hand
he has her phone.
He offers it up to her.
Something like a smile
playing around his buck teeth.

"Take it and stay,
listen and play."

He purrs.

BULLDOZE

The Memory comes bulldozing in
the call on that phone.
The call I never wanted to receive.

I always thought he'd get better
always hated the hospital
always taking Mum away with work
and now wanting Dad.

It wasn't going to have me too.
My father wasn't a hospital man.
Never one for indoors
and corridors and harsh lights.
I only wanted to see him in his element
climbing trees
covered in bark and pollen.
Laughing as he shook
the sawdust from his hair.

So the hospital visit
always felt wrong.

The Memory comes bulldozing in
the thin sound of my mother
calling from the hospital.
Saying he had gone.

The axe chop in my chest
the uprooting of my world
the endless winter
of never saying goodbye.
The frost of regret
unable to thaw.

Or that's how I remember feeling.
The feeling is different now.
As a tree I see it all from height,
incredible height.
It's just one memory in hundreds, thousands.
One memory in a pollen storm of memories
of Dad,
of laughter and love and joy.

One memory in an eternity of spring buddings
of Mum and Dad
loving me, smiling and comforting me.
Just one memory
among so many
that make my heartwood glow
that make my leaves unfurl
that make me yearn for sunlight and cool rain.

Memories I'd forgotten,
memories I've been too scared to remember,
memories I thought would bring too much pain.
Memories I had drowned out in anger
and the replaying of a message
a replaying of guilt Dad wouldn't want me to feel,
the scrolling of regret Mum doesn't want me to own.

The Memory comes bulldozing in
but with it burns a forest fire of others
far brighter, far hotter, far more real
far more in need of my attention.
Memories alight with my family's love.

CRUSHING

The phone was tiny
in her huge hands
its square black screen
a glazed stare sharing nothing.

Nothing to like.
Nothing to listen to.
Nothing to click.
Nothing to swipe.
Nothing to replay.

In that nothing
a sort of calm.

"I don't need to listen
because I hear him
with the heartwood of me."

A calm that she liked.
A calm that revealed the tweets of birds.
A calm that clicked.
Calmly she swiped
at Hoc.
Held him tight
in her monstrous grip.

His small beady
eyes frantic
as he scratched
and heaved
against her forested grip.

His smell
no more than a whiff
his face a Picasso of pain and pity.

Daphne tightened her grip,
until cracking was heard,
until all life was drained,
until the stare was shattered.
Until she felt the reassuring pop
as her phone was crushed.

UPGRADE

The phone.
A crumpled pile
all wires and shards and dust.
The line is dead. Her hand empty.
Hoc vanished.

WALKING BACK

Walking back
Daphne found that birds
began to perch in her crown.

Rabbits and deer
bounded and hopped
alongside her.
She felt the tickle of insects
scuttling around her branches.

She saw this forest
for the first time
as somewhere beautiful.
Its depth unrolling endlessly
in every shade of green,
every shadow of wonder.

Life hummed around her
in the croaking of far-off frogs
and the fluttering
of innumerable butterflies and moths
as the sky rolled into dawn.

Walking as a tree felt easy and free
but already she could feel her limbs hardening,
could feel the desire to be rooted
rising in her.

And if she was to be a tree
she wanted to grow near a friend.

SORRY

I was a bit mean to a friend
I said a few things to offend
if I can, then I must
re-sow this lost trust
and pray that our friendship can mend.

SAY SORRY

I fought my way out of apologising,
rains turned the ground to marsh.
The only hope is compromising.
We both said things considered harsh.

Rains turned the ground to marsh.
He was as much to blame as me.
I said things considered harsh.
It takes two to set an argument free.

Was he as much to blame as me?
Only I can decide what words follow.
It takes guts to set an argument free.
Say sorry today for a better tomorrow?

I must decide what words will follow.
I need to protect what could be lost.
I'll say sorry today for a better tomorrow.
A simple gesture is a worthwhile cost.

Horribly aware of what could be lost.
Hope is not built on compromise.
A simple gesture, a gladly given cost.
I've thought of a way to apologise!

ENTWINE TO ONE

I'll stay here beside you
however the weather blows.
Through harshest sun and deepest snows
we'll see the seasons through.

We'll share this field of view
our friendship newly sowed.
I'll stay here beside you
however the weather blows.

Loneliness won't rock you,
we'll share every tomorrow,
we'll prune out every sorrow.
We'll entwine to one statue,
I'll stay here beside you.

FRIENDSHIPS ARE BUILT ON SACRIFICE

Friendships are built on sacrifice
but what friend would allow the chop?
You say you'll stay with me and rot?
Sit summer's boil and winter's ice?

You'd risk it all, swallow the dice
commit to hobble-breath and stop.
Friendships are built on sacrifice
but what sort of friend would allow the chop?

Your committed heart will suffice.
A downpour does not require every raindrop,
a friendship is growth not harvest crop,
through you I wish to taste life's spice.
No friendship is built on sacrifice.
No worthy friend would allow the chop.

FEELiNG HUMAN

I fell asleep,
my head could fill a room
rough and unbending.

I fell asleep,
thinking how things had changed,
how I would never change.

Thoughts blocking out
all light.
Arms wrapped tight
in woody comfort.

I woke up,
my head was light
small and soft.

I woke up,
everything had changed.

Thoughts flittered
in bright sunlight,
hands pressing down
on soft warm earth
pushing me up
to standing.

A FRIENDSHIP NECKLACE

How did I ever
see him as a monster?

Euan is high above me
smiling his woody smile.
The light through his leaves
speaks of the cathedrals
we visited with school.

My twigs have poked to fingers,
my branches flexed to arms,
my roots stepped to feet.

"You're human again."

His laugh is like
waves crashing
and sea-sprayed winds.

As he laughs, something falls.

I pick up a nut
the size of a fist.

"Is this one of your dreams?"
I ask.

He nods — eyes amber-sad.

"A dream of you returning."

The nut, the seed
starts to move.

From its sides emerge
two curling vines,
from either side
their ends tangle
to form a loop.

Euan places the sprouted seed
necklace around my neck.

"Carry me with you."

he whooshes.

A GUARDIAN BORN

His whooshes become booms
as the ground starts to move.

His roots start to beat
as they wriggle like feet.

He shakes from the ground
his action astounds.

He moves as a tree
but mobile and free.

He towers so tall
his might will enthral.

A guardian of good.
A new protector for this wood.

THE WAY BACK

The way back
is always easier.

Feeling new life
in my legs
I run
past the rundown hut
of distractions.

But it had changed,
its technological ensnarements
now blanketed
in thick green moss.

Daphne sped the trail
that was once well worn
but now bloomed ahead of her,
its litterings
bursting forth into bright yellow
Narcissus and Primula.
The sad trails of sweets
and photos and toys
sinking into the earth
replaced by swooping grasses
and puffy white mushrooms.

Daphne sped the trail
before it disappeared,
into the belly
of a huge stump of
a warped old oak.

She was in the tunnel
on all fours crawling fast
for behind her the light was fading
the tunnel growing shut.
Up ahead
the happy warm glow
of the library seemed so far
and the tunnel was closing so quick,
creaking growing wood
so fast on her heels.

The jagged opening of the bookcase
through which she had crawled
was ahead,
mere feet away.
She reached for it.

And fresh grown wood
clamped around
her dirty white trainer.

MUM

A hand
snatched her up,
pulled her through.

Stood her up,
dusted her off
in the warm forest light
of the library.

She stands:
gob-smacked,
dumbfounded,
trainer missing.

As the librarian smiles,
she notices how
his front teeth
stick out more than the others.
How his hair rustles like leaves,
how his eyes are like amber.

*"You have to be careful
in these old libraries,"*

he says.

There is a kindness in his eyes,
of the wisdom of books
and the lessons of hard learning.

*"There is someone
here looking for you."*

The librarian gestures
to the huge oak
front desk.

Where her mother
is wringing rain from her hair.
It feels like too long
since she saw her
since she noticed her
since she carved out the time
to look at her.

Her mum looks cool
in her bright yellow mac
her hair looks funky
her eyes look tired.

Daphne runs to her
her eyes a river
her arms needing
to embrace her mother.

A CLEARING IN THE FOREST

I've been worried sick
I was calling
You weren't picking up
Are you ok?

I thought something had happened
I couldn't get hold of you
I was thinking the worse
Are you sure you're ok?

I know things have been tough
I'm sorry about the key
You were right to get angry
It won't happen again
As long as you're OK?

I'm sorry Mum
I lost my phone
I'm sorry Mum
I'm fine.

It's OK Mum
It's really fine
I'm sorry Mum
Don't worry Mum
I love you.

I'm ok ok Mum,
It won't happen again
I'm fine now
I'm with you.

What!

You...

I...

Oh love.

I love you too.

I love you too.

I love you too.

I'm sorry.

I love you too.

I love you too.

I love you too.

I love you too.

I'm sorry.

I love you too.

I love you too.

I love you too.

I love you too.

I love you too.

I'm sorry.

I love you too.

I love you too.

I love you too.

I love you too.

I love you too.

I love you too.

I love you too.

JOSEPH COELHO is the Waterstones Children's Laureate 2022-24 and a multi-award-winning author and poet. His debut poetry collection, *Werewolf Club Rules*, won the CLiPPA Poetry Award 2015. It was followed by *Overheard in a Tower Block*, selected for Empathy Lab's Read for Empathy listing, and *The Girl Who Became a Tree*, shortlisted for the CILIP Carnegie Medal 2021. Joseph is also the author of bestselling picture books. *Luna Loves Library Day* was voted one of World Book Day's top picture books to share while *If All the World Were...* won the Independent BookShop Week Book Award. Joseph Coelho works regularly with performance organisation Apples and Snakes and has performed poems for BBC TV, Channel 4, Blue Peter and CBeebies. His plays for young people have been performed by Little Angel, Polka and Unicorn theatres. He is a staunch ambassador for Britain's libraries and for diverse and inclusive new voices in poetry. He is also a National Poetry Day Ambassador. He lives in Kent.

www.thepoetryofjosephcoelho.com

KATE MILNER studied Illustration at Central St Martin's and has an MA in Children's Book Illustration from Anglia Ruskin University. She won the V&A Illustration Award in 2016 and the Klaus Flugge Prize in 2018 for *My Name is not Refugee*. She was longlisted for the Kate Greenaway Award with *The Girl Who Became a Tree* and shortlisted with *It's a No Money Day*. Kate is passionate about libraries. She is involved with every kind of activity from Storytime for toddlers to teen reading groups.

www.katemilner.com